For C. J. and Rebecca,
a couple o' flapjacks
—Tamson

For my friend and editor, Paula,
who kept me on the beam
—Stephen

Thanks to Margie, for her
hearty contribution to this book.



ISBN 0-439-72756-1


Published by Scholastic Inc., 557 Broadway, New York, NY 10012, by arrangement with Harcourt, Inc.


12 11 10 9 8 7 6 5 4 3 2 5 6 7 8 9 10/0

Printed in the U.S.A. 40

First Scholastic printing, February 2005

The illustrations in this book were created in pastel, pencils and watercolor.

The type was set in Cooper Black.

Designed by Scott Piehl

# Hey, Pancakes!

**WORDS BY**

## Tamson Weston

**PICTURES BY**

## Stephen Gammell

**SCHOLASTIC INC.**
New York  Toronto  London  Auckland  Sydney
Mexico City  New Delhi  Hong Kong  Buenos Aires

**Rrrrrrriiiiiinnnnnggggg . . . WHACK!**
**Shhhhh, alarm clock.**

**No shoe, holey sweater,
where's that other sock?**

**Why get up,
for goodness' sake?**

**Wait … that smell …
could it be … ? Pancakes!**

**Sift, stir,
whir, whisk,**

**Drop it in the pan,
and listen to it hiss.**

**A speck of this,
a few of those,**

**a flick of the wrist,
and up it goes.**

**A pancake flip,
a pancake flop,**

**pancake bottom
over pancake top.**

A pancake here,
a pancake there.

**One in the pan,
and three in the air.**

I'm flap Jack
in the hotcake seat.

**Check out the stack
that I'm gonna eat.**

**Holy cow!
It's pancake art!**

**Get ready, get set,
'cause here's the best part...**

**Add some butter and syrup
and—surprise!**

**Shazzam! It disappears right before your eyes!**

**Bite it in the middle—
it's a pancake hole.**

**If you want to pass,
pay the pancake toll.**

**Jelly in my ears,
syrup on my toes,**

**Hey, that's a blueberry
stuck on my nose.**

**Move over, Rover,
that last bite's mine.**

**All done now.
It's cleanup time.**

**Bye, sticky hands.**
**See ya, sticky face.**

Save some for later
in a secret place.

**With a little dab of maple behind each ear,**

**go out into the world and give a pancake cheer!**

# Grandma's Pancakes

| | |
|---|---|
| 1 | egg |
| 1 1/4 | cups buttermilk |
| 2 | tablespoons vegetable oil |
| 1 1/4 | cups flour |
| 1 | tablespoon sugar |
| 1 | teaspoon baking powder |
| 1/2 | teaspoon baking soda |
| 1/2 | teaspoon salt |
| | butter for frying |

In a medium-sized bowl, using a fork, mix together flour, sugar, baking powder, baking soda, and salt.

In a small bowl, beat the egg with the buttermilk and vegetable oil.

Make a well in the dry ingredients and pour in the wet ingredients. Stir gently until just blended (the batter will be lumpy).

Heat a pan and add a little butter. When the butter sizzles, pour a few spoonfuls of batter into the pan.

When the top of the pancake is bubbly, flip it! Fry the other side until the pancake is cooked all the way through (just a minute or so).

Serve immediately with your favorite topping.

*And remember to wash your hands before mixing, and leave the cooking to the big kids, please. Love, Grandma*